The Travelers Detective Club

PORTUGAL

SUSSI VOAK

ISBN -13 978-1-7340093-0-9

Cover illustration/chapter heading design by S. M. Savoy

DEDICATION

For Andre. May you always embrace the magic around you and believe in the magic that you are.

Table of Contents

Prologue

It was time once again. Travis walked into his boss's large corner office with windows overlooking the city, rays of sunlight fighting through the morning fog. He glanced up to the eagle on the top shelf that stood with a dignified grace not typically associated with a stuffed animal. Its yellow eyes followed Travis as he entered the room.

"Ma'am, has Baako been awake long?" Travis asked, turning toward the gray-haired woman sitting behind the large oak desk.

"Since this morning. It should be anytime now. Did you bring the files?"

Nodding, Travis handed her a thick manila folder as she rose from her chair.

"Close the door, please." Taking out the files she laid the papers side by side on the floor, each displaying a child's picture in the top right hand corner. "Now, we wait."

Moments later, Baako rustled her feathers, causing a thread to dislodge and float down to the floor. Travis and his boss sat waiting, eyes never leaving the strand. In a flurry of activity, the strand divided and then multiplied, transforming into a hand-sized stuffed animal.

"Most peculiar," Travis remarked.

"Yes. The magic buddies are getting more interesting each time."

From above, Baako nodded and turned her head ever so slightly, controlling the animal on the floor as it rolled across the papers.

After ten seconds of rolling around, the magic buddy lay still. The gray-haired woman waited a moment longer before retrieving the paper under the stuffed animal. "Jeremy Johnson. Age 11. His mom works in our computer research and design division."

"Shall I send a box?"

Nodding, she glanced up at the shelf and smiled as the eagle turned to her and winked.

1. The Box

With feet firmly planted on the skateboard, Jeremy rounded the corner and glided to a stop in front of his house. He flipped the board up with a tap of his foot, catching it in one hand, while un-strapping the buckle to his helmet with the other. He spotted a small brown box resting on the front porch. As he jogged up the steps, Jeremy was surprised to see his name typed in bold letters on the front.

Once inside, Jeremy wasted no time opening the box, which was so light it felt empty. It held a round, orange stuffed creature and a note, typed on thick parchment with the emblem TDC in golden letters at the top.

"Dear Jeremy,

Welcome to the Travelers Detective Club. You have been chosen as a member of a secret organization that dates back to a time when magic was an accepted part of everyday life. As a Travelers Detective, you will be asked to solve mysteries that can only be unraveled by those with magic buddies, one of which is enclosed with this letter. Your buddy will assist you in ways too many to list here. May magic guide you in your travels."

The letter was unsigned.

Jeremy grabbed the stuffed creature and turned it over in his hands. It was not much more than an orange ball of fur, with big beady eyes, short arms but large hands, no legs but feet and a tail. It had orange strands of hair that stuck straight up. On its back was a red trimmed patch with TDC in golden letters on a blue background, and a carabiner clip for attaching it to a bag. "What is this thing?" Jeremy muttered.

Jeremy grabbed the letter and box in his other hand, taking everything upstairs to his room. He read the letter a second time, searched the box in case he had missed something and stared at the magic buddy. "Well, what's so magical about you?" he asked it, but it just stared back at him. "Just what I thought. Must be a joke." Unable to ignore his growling stomach, he tossed the animal onto his bed and returned downstairs to raid the refrigerator. He was just digging into some leftover pizza when he heard the front door open and soon after his mom walked into the kitchen.

"Hi, Jeremy. Hey," his mom protested with what he knew to be a pretend scold, "that was going to be dinner."

"Don't you always say my job is to grow up and get big and strong?"

His mom smiled and put a bag of groceries on the counter. "Well, growing boy, why don't you run and get the rest of the groceries out of the car. Oh and by the way, I have some exciting news."

"What?"

"After the groceries."

Jeremy hopped off his stool, causing it to knock over the one next to it and they both went down with a crash.

"Jeremy!" Shaking her head, his mom turned to the pile of mail on the counter.

"Sorry, Mom," he said as he picked up the stools and dashed out the door, the stools still rocking from side to side.

Returning with the groceries, he began emptying the contents into the fridge. "So?"

"First tell me at least one thing about your day."

"Mom!" Jeremy stuffed two gallons of milk onto the top shelf of the fridge and slammed it shut.

"Go on."

Sighing, Jeremy thought for a moment. "I got an A on my math test."

"Nice," she said, giving him a high five.

"Now will you tell me?" Jeremy paused, holding a loaf of bread in his hand.

"We're going to Portugal!" she said with a smile.

"Sweet! When? Wait. Why Portugal?"

"Right after school gets out. My boss called me into her office today and said that as a reward for all my hard work the company was sending us on a trip and that's where the company has a rental."

"Way to go, Mom! Um, Where's Portugal?"

"Southern Europe. Do you know where Spain is?"

"Sure," Jeremy answered.

"It's right next door. We can look at a map later. But now you get to help me figure out what to make for dinner."

2. The Magic Buddy

Two hours later Jeremy was upstairs trying to do his homework. Distracted by the neighbor's barking dog, he caught sight of the box and magic buddy on his bed. Curious, he reached for the orange creature, turning it over in his hands. He moved its arms up and down and flipped it over to look at the patch on the back. TDC. Jeremy picked up the letter and read it a third time. TDC. Travelers Detective Club. "But what am I supposed to do with you?" Puzzled, he absentmindedly squeezed it in his hand.

An unfamiliar voice shouted, "Really, you can stop NOW!"

Jeremy jumped back, dropping it onto the bed. With eyes wide, he retreated toward his desk.

The magic buddy rolled over and came up on his feet. "Finally. I thought you'd never figure that one out. Well, did you? Or were you just guessing? And I thought Baako paired me with a smart one, but no."

It hopped from one foot to the other before doing a backflip.

"Ouch!" Jeremy banged into his desk chair as he stumbled further from his bed. Off balance, his arm knocked a container of pens off the desk and they crashed onto the floor. His heart racing, Jeremy sidestepped toward the door, his eyes never leaving the stuffed animal.

"Jeremy! Everything all right up there?" his mom called from downstairs.

"Uh, yeah Mom, sorry," he called down. "It talks! This thing can talk! What the heck?" Jeremy's hand gripped the doorknob.

"Of course I can talk. But who are you talking to?"

"What is going on?" Jeremy continued. "Dreaming, I must be dreaming," he said, pinching himself.

"Who are you talking to?" the animal asked.

"This can't be happening. Am I going crazy? Maybe I ate too much?"

"Helloooooooooo. Anybody in there?" the magic buddy exclaimed.

Jeremy stopped talking to himself, addressing the creature on the bed instead. "Uh, who are you? And how can you talk, if you don't have a mouth?"

"That depends on what you name me, now doesn't it? Wait, what? Of course I have a mouth."

"No, you don't."

The orange creature reached up, searching his face. After a pause, it said, "Guess I don't need one."

"What are you?" Jeremy asked.

"What, are you dense? Didn't you read your letter? I'm a magic buddy! Duh!"

"Why don't you stop with the attitude? I know you're a magic buddy. But what is a magic buddy?"

Not responding, it ran circles on the bed, then jumped up and down on Jeremy's pillow.

"I asked you a question!" Jeremy said, his voice rising.

"What's that, Jeremy? I didn't hear you," his mom called out from downstairs.

"Nothing, Mom," he responded as it did back flips across the bed.

"Hello!" Jeremy insisted. "Are you going to answer me? Hello!"

There was still no response.

Jeremy thought for a moment. "Thing. Hey, Thing. That's your name now. What is a magic buddy?"

The orange creature stopped and turned to look at Jeremy. "Really? Really? That's what you're going to name me?"

A smile spreading across his face, Jeremy nodded.

"Why, Baako, why?" Thing said, rolling his eyes.

"Now, can you please tell me what you are?" Jeremy asked as he sat down on his desk chair.

"Okay. So I'm supposed to help you solve puzzles when you travel, though..." Thing paused for a second as if wondering if he really would choose to be helpful. "When there are other people around I am supposed to stay quiet and just change colors. Blue if there's a clue nearby, yellow if you're walking away from a clue, red if there's another magic buddy around, purple if you're in danger or something's wrong."

"What kind of clues? What am I supposed to figure out?"

"How should I know? I'm just a 'thing,' remember?"

"Well, if you're not going to be helpful, I guess I could just turn you back off."

A look of concern came over Thing's eyes. "You wouldn't."

"Try me," Jeremy replied, standing up and reaching for Thing.

Thing caused a racket as he hopped from the headboard to a shelf and knocked over a model plane that crash-landed onto the floor. A muffled sound emanated from Thing.

"What was that?" Jeremy asked.

"That was me sticking my tongue out at you if I had a tongue, or a mouth."

Jeremy grabbed his desk chair, hopped onto it, and reached to snatch Thing who jumped out of the way, bouncing off the bed before disappearing underneath it.

Dropping to the floor, Jeremy reached under the bed, moving his arm from side to side, grasping at air. Frustrated, he sat up and leaned his back against his bed.

"This must be a joke," he murmured.

From underneath the bed came a barely audible reply. "It's not."

"Really? Cause it sure feels like it."

"I'll come out if you promise you won't turn me off."

There was a pause before Jeremy replied, "Are you going to tell me what this is all about? Cause if not I'm going to pack you in the box and send you back to wherever you came from."

"Yeah, yeah, okay. Just don't turn me off."

"And you have to be quiet around Mom and other people."

"I know that! Think I'm stupid or something?"

"So, do we have a deal?"

Waddling out from under the bed, Thing looked up at Jeremy and nodded, which was more like a bow as he didn't have a head.

"What is the Travelers Detective Club? What kind of clues are we supposed to find? And why me? And-"

"Hold on," Thing interrupted. "I was just born yesterday."

"I think you've got that wrong. The saying goes I wasn't just born yesterday and people say it when--"

"Stop!" Thing interrupted again. "I mean it. I was just born yesterday. So I don't know the answers to all your questions. I was told I'm to help you in any way I can. And I'm supposed to make sure no one figures out that I'm magical."

"You're magical? What can you do?"

Thing stared at Jeremy. And waited.

"Oh right."

"I was told you were bright but I'm beginning to wonder."

"Hey, give me a break. It's not every day a magical blob wanders into my life and starts talking and jumping around."

"Did you just call me a blob?" Thing asked, his voice rising as his eyes grew wider.

As Thing began to tremble, Jeremy thought it best to make nice. "Sorry." Quickly turning back to his original questions, Jeremy asked, "Do you know why I was chosen?"

"I only know that Baako does the choosing. He's the original magic buddy. And I know that adults can't be picked. They tend not to believe in magic so it was decided long ago to keep them out of this whole business."

"So, what's our first problem that we have to solve?" Jeremy asked.

"How should I know? I can't figure out everything for you."

"Wait. It's the Travelers Detective Club, right?"

"Uh, yeah."

Ignoring Thing, Jeremy went on. "My mom just told me we're going to Portugal in a couple of days so I guess we'll find out soon."

***

The next few days flew by with Jeremy busy with school and his mom getting ready for the trip. For the most part, the time was uneventful except for the first day Jeremy got back from school after Thing came home in the mail. Upon entering his bedroom, he was welcomed to a disaster. His clothes had been emptied from his drawers and strewn about his room, so had the contents of his desk.

Furious, he stared up at Thing who was perched on the highest shelf in his room. "That," Thing stated, "is for calling me a blob."

3. Surprise On The Plane

"What are you doing? You can't put me in another box!" Thing bounced around Jeremy's room, from bed to shelves to his desk and around again with Jeremy chasing him.

"Jeremy, we have to get going now!" his mom yelled from downstairs.

"I know, just a second. Thing, we have to go!"

"I'm not going unless you keep me out of that zippered box," Thing said, backing away from the edge of the top shelf.

"It's called a suitcase."

"Whatever. Keep me out of it."

"Okay, okay. I'll clip you to my backpack but you have to stay quiet," Jeremy promised.

"Works for me," Thing said, hopping down from the shelf and onto Jeremy's extended hand. "Where are we going next?" he asked as Jeremy clipped him to the dark blue bag.

"To the car so we can drive to the airport."

"I want to see out the window."

"I'm not holding you up so you can look out the window."

"If you don't, I'll…"

"You'll what?" Jeremy asked, with raised eyebrows. "You have to be quiet, remember."

"I wouldn't dream of talking…" Thing paused. "But I can make farting noises and your mom will think it's you. Or the people on the plane will…"

"Okay, okay. I'll prop you up on a bag or something so you can look outside. Jeez."

Running down the stairs, his pack on his back, Thing bobbed up and down. "Weeeeeee," Thing whispered.

"Shush!"

"Finally. Come on Jeremy, I don't want to miss our flight!"

"Mom. When have we ever been late for anything? You always give us extra time, remember?"

Smiling, she pointed to Thing as they walked toward the car. "Is that new?"

"What? Oh that? Yeah. It's the new cool thing at school."

Giving it one more glance as she unlocked the car, she added, "It's a bit weird looking, isn't it?"

"I hear you on that," Jeremy snickered. He glanced down at Thing whose eyes had gone wide again as he opened the car door and got into the back seat.

"Ffffffffffffffffffffffffffftt!"

"Jeremy! Really!" his mom said eyeing him through the rear view mirror.

"Sorry, Mom." Jeremy glared at Thing.

"Did you remember your computer?" his mom asked as he continued what had turned into a staring contest with Thing.

"Of course."

"What about the pile of underwear I left on your bed?"

"Mom!" he exclaimed, turning away from Thing and meeting her eyes in the mirror.

"Okay, okay. We're off, then."

The drive to the airport was uneventful as Jeremy found a way to prop his backpack onto one of the other bags so Thing had a full view out the window.

After checking in for the flight, they made their way to the deserted boarding area. "See, Mom. I told you we were going to be early. We're the first ones here."

"Better to be early than miss the flight." His mom put her bags down on one of the plastic chairs. "Do you mind staying here while I go to the bathroom?"

Jeremy nodded, pulling out his computer from his bag, which he plopped down on the chair next to him.

A muffled sound came from under the backpack. Jeremy realized he had placed his bag on top of Thing. He quickly flipped it over so Thing was on top. "Sorry." Thing glowered at him.

On the computer, militants in white armor were racing through a battleship. From the corner of his eye Jeremy noticed Thing straining against the metal clip. "What are you doing?" Jeremy whispered.

In a barely audible voice Thing said, "I want to watch too."

"Okay but I don't have any earphones for you so you won't be able to hear."

"That's okay, I'll make up my own sounds."

Jeremy glared at him.

"Kidding, I'm kidding."

The waiting area slowly filled up. Sounds of families talking and little kids running around filtered through his headphones. Jeremy was relieved that Thing was content to watch the movie without bringing attention to himself. Soon after the movie ended, it was time to pack up and go.

While standing in line, Jeremy noticed a girl his age, standing in the back with her parents. She had a small red animal clipped to her backpack. It was a moment before Jeremy realized what he was looking at. He took his backpack off his shoulder and checked on Thing who had turned a deep, cardinal red. Jeremy turned back to look at the girl. She had a yellow bird on the front of her red t-shirt and her buddy, if it was that, appeared to be a type of bird with short pudgy legs, wings that stuck out and a beak that was a bit big for its body.

"Pretty soon you're going to be taller than me, you know," his mom was saying.

"Way taller," he smiled, turning his attention away from the girl.

"But you'll always be my…"

"Don't say it," he joked as she rubbed the tight, black curls on top of his head.

"Are you going to keep your hair short or do you want to change it up a bit?"

"No, I like it this way. It's easier to manage."

Just before boarding the plane, Jeremy saw the girl with the bird buddy looking at him. He gave her a smile before hurrying to find his seat. Reaching number 38E near the back of the plane, a toy train displaying the number 28 on it was resting on his seat. His mom said, "Oh look, Tram 28."

"What's Tram 28?"

"It's the most famous tram in Lisbon. Its route goes through many of the key sites in the city. Who left it here? Someone from the last flight, perhaps?"

As his mom began unpacking her headphones and book, Jeremy examined the tram. Taped to the bottom was a folded-up piece of paper. He started to open the note and saw the golden TDC emblem emblazoned at the top. He let out a short gasp and glanced at his mom to see if she had noticed but she already had her headphones on. Jeremy shifted in his seat, pretending to look out the window while he removed the note and placed it inside a book he'd brought to read.

"Something valuable has disappeared. Only the horseman can bring it back. He needs you to find the four colored objects that

28

help him breathe. Castles, museums and playgrounds will give you what you need to complete this task."

Jeremy stuffed the note in the side of his seat and turned back to his mom, tapping her on the shoulder. She removed an earbud from her right ear.

"Mom, are there castles in Portugal?"

"Sure, several. I thought you might enjoy seeing some."

"Definitely," he replied, smiling to himself.

4. The Second Detective

The plane took off, rising quickly into the sky before leveling off as Jeremy chewed a stick of gum, trying to keep his ears from popping. He searched for the girl with the funny looking bird. She was sitting with her parents on the other side of the plane, a middle section of seats between them. Jeremy's curiosity increased and he found it difficult to contain. He had to find out if she was part of the club.

"Mom, mind if I get up and walk around?"

"Of course not, go ahead," she responded, standing up to let him out of his seat before turning back to her book.

Jeremy walked down the girl's aisle, passing by her row on his way to the back of the plane. A moment after he reached the area near the bathrooms, the girl with the bird came up behind him.

He turned around. "Hi, I'm Jeremy."

"I'm Devon. Didn't you have a red, funny looking blob?"

"Right here." Jeremy continued in a whisper, "But please don't call him a blob, he'll get upset." He pulled Thing out of his pocket where he'd stuffed him before leaving his seat.

"Don't ever do that again!" Thing exclaimed, his eyes wide, as if trying to shoot lasers at Jeremy.

"What?"

"Stick me in your pocket. Don't do it again. Your pockets stink!"

Devon took a step back. "Wow, yours talks! How does he do that?"

"I just squeezed him by accident and he started talking. Doesn't yours?"

"No. But let me try."

"Um, why don't you go into the bathroom first. When he started talking he was pretty…animated."

Devon went into the bathroom, coming out a few moments later.

"That was fast. Did it work?" Jeremy asked.

"Yeah, but she didn't like the smell and asked me to leave. This is phenomenal," Devon said in a calm, measured voice.

"So are you a part of…" Jeremy paused, unsure what to say next. He remembered he wasn't supposed to tell anyone about the club.

Devon's bird spoke in a barely audible voice. "Yes." Both Thing and the bird turned orange.

"She started to tell me something about changing colors but then said she had to get out of the bathroom," Devon said. "Do they change colors, I mean, besides just now?"

"Yeah, they do, among other things," Jeremy replied. "They were both red because they were near each other. I can tell you about the rest later. Did you get a tram?" he asked.

"Yep. Did yours have a note?"

"Uh huh."

They were both silent for a moment. "Hey, we have an extra seat in our row," Jeremy said. "Wanna sit there?"

"Sure."

Walking back to his seat, Jeremy tapped his mom on the shoulder. "Mom, this is Devon. I met her in the back. Can she sit with us?"

"I don't see why not," she said. "But let's go check with Devon's parents first."

After Devon introduced her parents, Jeremy's mom spoke up. "Didn't I meet you at the Tech conference in Portland a few months back?" she asked Devon's dad.

"Oh yes, that's right." Stroking his mustache he asked, "You work for Tech too?"

"Yes, I do."

"Why don't you sit with us and the kids can have their own space," Devon's dad continued.

"Thanks Dad," Devon said.

As he and Devon were walking back to his row Jeremy heard, "Psst."

Jeremy glanced down at Thing, but turned away as he slid into his window seat.

"Psssssssst!"

"What?"

"Did you notice?" Thing said. "All the families here look alike."

"Uh, yeah."

"Why don't you and your mom match?"

"Because…" Jeremy paused. "I don't want to explain it right now."

"Why are you brown and everyone else is cream colored?" Thing continued.

"Go to sleep, Thing."

"But…"

"You're supposed to be quiet, remember?"

"Is he always so…animated?" Devon laughed.

"Yep." Jeremy waited for Devon to follow-up on Thing's comments but she didn't, so he continued. "You don't seem surprised that they can talk and move."

"They can move, too?"

"Yeah, he started doing back flips at first and then he destroyed my room for calling him a blob."

Devon snickered.

"Didn't yours move in the bathroom?" Jeremy asked.

"No. She just asked to leave because of the smell."

"How can you act like this is normal?"

"I don't know. They're called magic buddies so I just assumed they would be magical."

"Does anything get you excited?" Jeremy asked, a quizzical look on his face.

"Sure. This whole trip is exciting."

Jeremy wondered if Devon would react if her bird started flying around the plane and was beginning to think she wouldn't.

5. Turbulence

"Can I see your note?" Jeremy asked.

"Sure." She pulled a piece of paper from her jean's pocket. The two notes were identical. "Do you think we're supposed to work together?"

"Yeah, I guess," Jeremy said. "But how would that work? Wouldn't we have to travel together?" Suddenly the plane dropped and shuddered. The seat belt sign dinged on.

Jeremy felt a kick in his side. "What?"

"What's happening?" Thing whispered.

"Oh. Just a bit of turbulence. When the plane hits an air pocket it can bounce around."

"We're on a plane?" Both Jeremy and Devon looked down at Devon's magic buddy who had been quiet up until now.

"Yes, we're on a plane. We're flying across the ocean to Portugal," Devon answered.

"You mean we're up in the sky and flying?" The bird's voice seemed to be shaking.

"Of course," Devon replied.

"So, how can we convince our parents to travel together?" Jeremy continued.

"I'm not sure." Devon's gaze was slow to leave her buddy. "What do you and your mom have planned for the trip?"

"Well…" Caught off guard, Jeremy realized he didn't know much about the trip. His mom had been on him to keep up with his schoolwork and he had been trying to teach himself how to write computer games. "We're going to see a castle or two, and my mom mentioned this tram," he said pointing to the one on his lap.

The plane lurched again.

"Weeeee," Thing squealed quietly.

Jeremy noticed Devon glance down at her magic buddy.

"What does purple mean?" Devon asked.

"What?" Jeremy said.

"What does it mean if our magic buddies turn purple?"

Jeremy paused. "It means there's danger or something is wrong. Why?"

"Because she's purple." Devon said holding up her buddy.

Jeremy looked down at Thing who was still orange. "Mine is still orange. Is there something wrong?" he asked, addressing Thing.

"No. Though I wish the plane would dance more."

"What's wrong?" Devon asked her buddy.

But her bird had closed her eyes and seemed to have gone to sleep. Shrugging, Devon turned back to Jeremy. "I know for sure we're going on the tram," she said matter-of-factly. And there's a science museum I really want to see. Do you like science?"

"Depends. Not so much if I have to listen to my teacher go on and on, but doing experiments and stuff, yeah."

The plane bumped up and down for several seconds. "Weeeee," Thing said again but Jeremy glared at him and he stopped.

"There are also several castles that we plan on seeing," she continued.

Jeremy began to think he could have helped his mom out a bit more. He noticed Devon watching him, expectantly.

"What?" he asked.

"I asked you a question but you seem lost in space."

"Oh, sorry. What was your question?"

"Where are you staying?"

"I'm not sure." Jeremy began to feel self conscious about not knowing what his mom had planned for the trip. "All I know is her work has a rental somewhere in Lisbon, which is why we're going to Portugal."

"Hey, that's why we're going too!" Devon exclaimed. "Ours is near Rossio square. I wonder if our apartments are close to each other."

Feeling his face get warm, Jeremy quickly got up. "Let me go check." He walked around to where their parents were sitting, noticing they were deep in conversation. They stopped as he approached.

"Everything okay, Jeremy?" his mom asked.

"Oh yeah. Where are we staying when we get to Lisbon?"

"My company has a small apartment near Rossio Square."

Devon's dad, sitting in the window seat, spoke up. "Really? Tech must have two apartments nearby. What street are you on?" he asked, pulling a map from his seat back pocket.

"Great," Jeremy said, leaving them to talk.

"Well, it looks like we're staying in the same part of the city at least," he said to Devon once he returned to his seat.

Devon began twirling the end of her shoulder length hair in her fingers, lost in thought.

Just then the flight crew handed out dinner. Devon spoke up after they started eating. "How about we see if we can all ride the tram together tomorrow. That would be a start."

6. The Tram

The next morning, Jeremy was looking through his suitcase for some snacks when his mom said, "Jeremy, breakfast will be ready in a minute."

"I know," he replied, opening a granola bar. Taking a bite, he said, "Mom, what do you think about traveling a bit with Devon and her parents? It would be fun having someone my age to hang out with."

"We are taking the tram together today. After that, I don't know. Let's take it day by day. It would be nice to have company but I'd like to spend some time just with you, too."

After a breakfast of fried eggs, bacon and toast, Jeremy and his mom walked around the corner to meet Devon and her parents outside their apartment. Jeremy eyed laundry hanging off black, wrought iron balconies and the yellow and white concrete buildings four stories high covered with soot. Devon wore another shirt with a bird on the front, and Jeremy couldn't help remarking, "I guess you like birds."

"And…" she answered.

He quickly said, "It's a nice shirt."

She glanced at him suspiciously.

"What?"

"Nothing," Devon replied. "Let's go." And together both families walked toward the tram stop. In the cool morning, bakery owners and coffee shopkeepers were hosing down the cobblestones, the smell of pastries mixing with the petrol of the taxis and trucks passing by. Electrical wires hung overhead, framing the stone street embedded with steel trolley tracks.

They arrived just as the tram came, looking just like the toy they had found on their plane seats. It had the same yellow base atop which windows were lined, giving full views of the passing streets. A steel cable reached up to connect to the tangle of electrical lines hovering overhead. "The numbers on the trams are route numbers, just like buses at home," Jeremy's mom said.

The tram wound up and around narrow streets, lined with apartment buildings, shops and restaurants. Ten minutes into the ride, they were at a standstill as someone had double parked their car and there wasn't room for the tram to pass. While they were waiting, Jeremy realized he hadn't been paying attention to Thing. Hanging from his backpack, clipped by a miniature carabiner, he was still orange, and glaring at Jeremy. "What?"

"You know I want to see outside!" Thing scolded.

Jeremy turned his backpack sideways so Thing could look out and then said to Devon, "We need to make sure to notice if our buddies change color."

"You were going to tell me what other colors mean, remember."

"Not here on the tram," he replied. "Later."

"Sure," Devon said. "But just so you know yours hasn't changed colors. Neither has Birdbrain."

"Birdbrain?" Jeremy started to laugh but stopped when he saw Devon scowling at him. "You're right. I shouldn't laugh. I named mine Thing."

Now it was Devon's turn to laugh.

A sound like a muffled raspberry came from Thing. Jeremy glared at him while Devon chuckled. Birdbrain was quiet. In fact, Jeremy hadn't heard a peep out of her.

The double parked car moved and they continued up the hill, becoming more crowded with each stop. "We're off next," Devon's mom said five minutes later.

They got off at Portas do Sol, or Gates to the Sun in English. Taxis, trams and tuk tuks drove by, honking their horns and striking their bells. Five musicians were playing guitars and drums off to one side while multiple nearby churches rang their bells minutes apart. The smell of cigarette smoke filled the air. A square laid out before them, providing a view of red tiled roofs and a wide river below. The road and sidewalks were so narrow that buses weren't allowed and at times pedestrians had to step into the road to let each other pass.

Jeremy's tendency was to hurry on the short walk around the corner and up a hill to the castle but the way was crowded. People were spilling into the street and Jeremy's mom had to remind him several times to stay on the sidewalk as multiple cars came up the hill behind them. They passed people selling various things: selfie sticks, necklaces made of large beads, paintings of the castle.

Jeremy noticed a sign on the sidewalk outside a café advertising ice cream.

"Mom…"

"After the castle," she said.

Once they arrived at Saint George's Castle and purchased their tickets, Jeremy and Devon ran ahead.

"Okay, tell me about the colors," Devon said.

"So, you know about red, which means another buddy is around, and purple, which means danger." They walked over a drawbridge while Jeremy continued. "The others are blue, for when a clue is nearby and yellow means you're walking away from a clue." They walked into an open courtyard. "Do you think we'll find something here?" Jeremy asked.

"I sure hope so." Devon replied. "That would be a great way to start the trip. Where are you from, anyway?"

"Oakland, California, near San Francisco. What about you?"

"Portland, Oregon. I'll be in the sixth grade next year. You?"

"Same," he replied.

"Are you excited about middle school?" Devon asked.

"Yeah, sure," Jeremy said without enthusiasm.

"You don't sound excited."

"Well... just starting in a new school. Don't know what to expect is all."

7. Saint George's Castle

Jeremy and Devon walked around exploring the castle. The sun reflected off the light-gray stones, stacked like oversized bricks. Running his fingers over the stone, Jeremy almost scratched his skin on the rocky surface. There were open courtyards and narrow, steep stairs leading up to walkways just wide enough for two people to pass if they turned sideways. Once up the stairs Jeremy and Devon gazed over the city and down onto people touring the castle below.

"I always wondered what these were called," Devon remarked as she peered through one of the gaps between the walls at the top of the castle.

"Battlements," Jeremy replied without hesitation, glancing over the edge. "The walls and towers were built by the Moors in medieval times," he explained. "They'd hide behind here, see, and shoot down at the enemy below." Jeremy mimicked pulling back on a bow and arrow. "Got him!" Devon shook her head, drawing her hand over her eyes as if embarrassed, as he continued. "But then the Christians invaded and took over, dedicating it to Saint George."

Devon peered at him quizzically before continuing. "What do you suppose used to be down there?" She pointed to the open courtyard.

"At one point a royal palace was down there but a couple of earthquakes…What?"

Devon was staring at him with a puzzled look on her face. "For someone who didn't know much about this trip you sure know a lot about this castle."

"Oh, I looked it up last night on my computer. I didn't have much time before we got to Portugal."

"And you remember it all, just like that?"

Jeremy shrugged. "We can go back and get a brochure if you want."

"No, that's okay. I don't need to know that much about a castle."

They continued exploring the grounds and came upon two mini-cannons. Jeremy squatted down to pretend to shoot one. Devon walked away, shaking her head.

"Psst." Jeremy looked around then turned his attention back to the cannon. "Pssssssst." Looking down at his side he noticed Thing was blue, not orange.

Jeremy quickly glanced around. Not finding anything he walked away from the cannon into the walkway, bustling with tourists.

Thing turned yellow. Jeremy headed back toward the cannon. Thing was blue again. He peered inside the cannon and saw a piece of paper. Grabbing it, he realized it was a pamphlet for a tour of more castles. Convinced it wasn't important, he put it back and walked away.

Thing turned yellow.

Returning to the cannon, Thing turned blue.

"Jeeezzz. How many times do I have to change colors? Why do I even bother?"

Ignoring Thing's remarks, Jeremy grabbed the paper. Thing became an even darker shade of blue. Devon had been reading a plaque before turning to witness Jeremy's back and forth. She questioned him as she approached. "What is it? What did you find?"

"I found it," whispered Thing.

"Yeah, well why don't you just tell me something's there instead of just turning blue?" Jeremy scolded.

"I'm supposed to be quiet remember? Plus, I don't know what you're looking for, my body just changes colors, okay!"

Turning his attention back to Devon, Jeremy showed her the brochure. It was an advertisement for a place called Sintra.

"More castles."

There was Estrada da Pena, or National Palace of Pena, which was painted with multiple bright colors. There was a second castle called Castle of the Moors that had a multitude of stairs and battlements. "Are we supposed to go there?" he asked.

"It would seem like it," smiled Devon, pointing to Birdbrain who had turned blue as well. "Those are actually on our list of things to see," she continued. As they walked away, having put the paper in his pocket, their buddies slowly changed back to orange.

Devon and Jeremy walked back over the castle's drawbridge and saw on their right a large grassy hill, rising from the base of the walls. Strutting on the grass as well as up on the path were three large, beautiful peacocks. Jeremy had never seen a peacock and was amazed at all the colors. Devon was fascinated by them. Walking up behind him she was unable to contain her excitement, exclaiming, "Wow, they are so beautiful! Their colors glimmer in the sunlight! I never knew I'd see peacocks here!" Lacking her enthusiasm, Jeremy continued toward the castle entrance. "Why do you think that one is pacing back and forth like that?" Devon asked.

Jeremy turned back to see Devon approach one of the peacocks. It appeared to be alternately staring at her and something at its feet. Devon reached down into the grass and grabbed something. Coming closer Jeremy saw a rectangular, grey stone resting in her hand. "What's that?" he asked.

"I'm not sure. Birdbrain is blue and I saw the peacock staring down at this but there are more and they all look the same," she said, almost tripping over her words as she noted other rocks on the ground. Devon gave Jeremy the stone. As she was talking he absentmindedly grabbed Thing.

"Whoa," Devon said.

The stone in Jeremy's hand had changed. It was now a light bluish, purplish stone.

"What the …" he started to say when Devon said, "Let go of Thing."

He did and the stone turned back to a dull, gray color. She put a hand around Birdbrain but nothing happened. She held out her hand and Jeremy gave her the stone. She then held on to Birdbrain and the stone became colorful once again.

"I guess our buddies are full of surprises," she grinned.

They both marveled at its color. Devon put it in her pocket and turned to see their parents coming over the drawbridge.

"Looks like these adventures are pretty easy," Jeremy said as he started to walk toward his mom.

"Uh Jeremy. Why is Thing purple? Is something wrong?"

"What are you talking about?" Peering down at his side, Thing had indeed turned purple. He glanced at Devon's side. "Um, Devon. Birdbrain is purple too."

"This can't be good," Devon whispered.

Scanning the grounds of the castle, he saw a man moving toward them in the shadows of the overhanging trees. His eyes were shielded by glasses but Jeremy sensed they were focused on him. Tall and dark, the man was an imposing figure. Jeremy's heart started pounding. Jeremy turned to Devon, whose eyes reflected the fear rising in his chest. "We need to leave!" he exclaimed.

They turned to run but bumped, instead, into an older woman. She was wearing a straw hat with a blue flower, her blondish grey hair sticking out from underneath. Her sunglasses hid her eyes. "Quick! Come with me," she insisted, flashing a TDC badge before promptly tossing it back in her purse.

She attempted to lead them toward the exit of the castle but Jeremy glanced at Devon and they both stopped. At the same time, Jeremy heard his mom calling him.

"We can't just go with you," he said.

"Yeah, what's going on?" Devon inquired.

"Plans have changed," the woman replied. "Someone is trying to sabotage your mission. They want the things you find for themselves, so they can do more harm. Meet me at the entrance to this castle when you have found all the objects and I will give you further instructions. You must meet me here in three days at noon. And stay away from that man," she said pointing to the dark figure approaching. "Don't talk to him. He will try and trick you."

With that she disappeared into the crowd while they ran to their parents. As they left the castle grounds, Jeremy turned back. The dark figure was standing still, watching them leave.

8. The Statue

"Did you like the castle?" Devon's mom asked Devon and Jeremy.

"Yes," they both said in unison. Jeremy turned to Devon whose eyes reflected his own concern. They almost walked right past the specialty shop but Devon's dad said, "Anyone up for some ice cream?"

As he sat at the table, Jeremy absentmindedly stirred what turned out to be gelato.

"Jeremy, what's wrong?" his mom asked.

He glanced at Devon, who was twirling her hair, not knowing what to say.

"We're both a little bummed," Devon said, covering for him. "I guess we both like traveling together and we know that after this we have to go our separate ways. It's nice having a friend when you're away from home."

Jeremy stared at her, amazed how fast she could think on her feet.

Her mom smiled and looking over at Jeremy's mom said, "Well, I'm not sure what will happen tomorrow but today isn't over yet. We talked about it when you were exploring the castle. There's a church within walking distance we wanted to see. How about we keep traveling together for now?"

Devon and Jeremy both smiled. Encouraged, Jeremy tasted his strawberry gelato for the first time.

"Jeremy says he likes science and would be interested in exploring the museum with us," Devon stated.

"And Mom, look at this pamphlet. These castles are on their list. Can we go too?" Jeremy asked.

Their parents laughed. "When we get back tonight," Devon's dad said, "we can decide what to do next."

"I would like to keep traveling with Devon, Mom."

"Yeah, please!" Devon pleaded.

"We'll see," she said with a smile.

They walked back down the hill, passing the tram stop on their way to the church, and ducked into a little store to buy some gum. As his mom handed it to Jeremy, he said, "Obrigado," to the shopkeeper. His mom was always on him to learn at least a few words of the local language. The shopkeeper asked his mom, "Is that your son?"

"Yes," she replied.

"But you have white skin and he has brown skin."

"That's the way it goes, sometimes," she said smiling.

While irritated at the shopkeeper, Jeremy appreciated how his mom answered people without giving up their story.

Turning to leave the store, Jeremy thought he glimpsed a tall, dark figure lurking in the shadows. However, when he glanced back over his shoulder, the man was gone. Thing's feet were purple, as they had been since leaving the castle but he decided not to tell Devon.

While walking up the hill Devon glanced over at Jeremy. "Does that happen much?"

"What, the shopkeeper? Yeah, it does. Either that or people stare."

Devon started to say something but stopped.

They finally reached the church set back at the edge of a courtyard and went inside. It was dark, quiet, and musty. Old statues of saints lined the walls, dimly lit by flickering candles and what light shone through a small, solitary stained glass window. Bored, Jeremy wandered outside, leaving the others to tour without him.

Sitting on a low stonewall he gazed over Lisbon to the water. "Sorry about that," Thing said, peeking up at Jeremy.

"About what?"

"The shopkeeper," Thing replied.

"Oh, thanks." Jeremy didn't feel up to talking. He looked, instead, at the view below. Red tile roofs covered the white concrete homes while lines of laundry fluttered in the gentle breeze. In the distance, there was a red bridge that appeared to be a replica of the Golden Gate Bridge back home in San Francisco. It was comforting for him, to be so far from home and yet be reminded of it.

Devon came out of the church. "Do you see what I see?" she asked.

"What?" Jeremy responded.

She pointed. "Down there. The statue of the soldier on the horse." Devon pointed to a large statue in the middle of a square below.

"Oh yeah, that's cool." He turned and pointed out in the distance. "Did you see the red bridge over there that looks just like the Golden Gate -"

Devon interrupted him. "Did you forget?"

"What?" He turned, dropping his arm. She stared at him, waiting. "Oh, the horseman! Do you think he's the one in the note?"

"Well, he is a man on a horse. And he's definitely not breathing," Devon replied.

9. Followed

"Wow, we have to get down there," Jeremy said. "How do we...?" He glared down at his side. "Stop kicking me, Thing!"

But Thing continued, pleading, "Let's go play down there!" while Jeremy tried to grab him.

Jeremy's hand froze in midair. "Where?" Peering around the side of the church, he spotted a large playground, many streets below, partially hidden in a grove of trees. It was in a large park, had a slide, a climbing structure and big green open space.

"Yeah, let's!" Birdbrain said, which startled both Jeremy and Devon, as she hadn't said much the entire trip.

"Sorry, guys, we're a bit old for that," Devon reminded them.

"I know Jeremy is a bit slow-," said Thing.

"Hey," Jeremy interrupted.

Ignoring him Thing continued, "But Birdbrain, I thought your person was a bit brighter. Should I remind them or would you like to?"

"Should we give them a clue?" the stuffed bird teased.

"Do you think it will help Devon 'cause I don't think it's much help to this guy."

"Okay, I've about had enough of you." Jeremy reached for Thing, but Thing bounced around frantically on his short leash. Right when Jeremy was about to grab him, the carabiner snapped off and Thing dashed to hide behind Devon.

"Okay you two, enough!" Devon reached behind her to grab Thing but he slid away from her grasp.

"Come on, Thing. People might start to notice," Devon said.

"Not unless he promises he won't turn me off."

Devon glanced questioningly at Jeremy. Sighing, he said, "Okay, okay."

As Devon picked up Thing and handed him over to Jeremy, Birdbrain spoke again. "Remember your riddle."

Glaring at Thing as he clipped him back on, Jeremy noticed Devon searching her pockets.

"Castles, museums and playgrounds will give you what you need to complete this task," Jeremy said.

Devon glanced up curiously.

"It's the last line of the riddle," he said.

"I remember now," she said, regarding him with interest.

"Do I get any credit for my memory?" he asked, addressing Thing, who didn't respond and turned his back.

"Well, it is a park," Devon said.

"And we found it by taking Tram 28," Jeremy added.

"We?" It was Thing again. Jeremy chose to ignore him while Devon chuckled.

"There are more things to find before we can help the horseman," Devon said. "Oh, wait. The woman said that plans have changed. What does that mean? We still have to get the objects to the horseman, right?"

"I guess...I'm not sure," Jeremy said uncertainly.

The square was becoming more crowded and Devon realized their Buddies had changed. "Hey, Birdbrain is more purple and so is Thing. We have to be extra careful."

Jeremy regarded the growing crowd and caught sight of the woman with the hat. As he continued to inspect the crowd his eyes stopped on a man, standing in the corner. Jeremy had seen him before at the castle. He remembered the single, diagonal, white stripe on his blue shirt and wondered if it was simply a coincidence. Perhaps all tourists went to the same places. Knowing their buddies were purple he tried to find the other man from the castle but couldn't.

"I don't like being followed," Devon complained, her tone hinting at both irritation and fear.

"Me neither," Jeremy agreed with a worried look. "But perhaps she's just trying to make sure we're safe."

"You're probably right," Devon said. "We need to convince our parents to let us go down to the playground. We have more things to find, and maybe there's something there."

When their parents came out of the church, Jeremy asked his mom, "Can we please go down there?"

"Aren't you guys a bit old for that?"

"We just want to run around a bit," Devon added.

"I'm okay with it." Looking at Devon's parents who nodded, she continued, "Let's go then."

10. The Bird

Jeremy and Devon raced down the sidewalk and around the church, until they reached the long staircase leading down to the park.

"Devon, wait!" her mom called out. "You need to stay where we can see you!"

Jeremy and Devon waited for their parents to catch up. "Sorry," Devon said to her mom.

"It's okay," she said, giving Devon a squeeze around the shoulders.

"What if we duck in and get a coffee while the kids play?" Devon's dad suggested, pointing to a café midway down the stairs with tables and chairs set up outside.

"Great idea," Jeremy's mom replied.

Jeremy and Devon raced down the stairs to a merry-go-round. Devon got on first and as she spun, Jeremy could see Birdbrain open her wings and catch some air. When it was Jeremy's turn, Thing let out a "Weeeeee," as they spun around. Getting off, Jeremy was still feeling dizzy when Devon nudged him. Raising his head, he saw a bird.

"What? Why are you pointing out a bird to me?" he asked Devon, as he turned to explore the rest of the park.

She grabbed his arm. "Wait," she said. "Have you seen a bird like that here?"

"What is it with you and birds?"

Ignoring his question, she explained. "This one's different. The others here are black like crows back home, not light blue. Do you see its bright orange legs and the streak of yellow on its tail feathers? And check out Birdbrain."

Birdbrain was flapping her wings. Also, she and Thing had both turned blue. The bird flew away and the Buddies turned orange. It came close and they were back to blue. "Oh wow!" Jeremy exclaimed!

"Do you like the color changes?" Thing asked, with a twinkle in his eyes, "'cause I can change more if you want," he said while flashing red, then green, then orange, blue, and purple in rapid succession.

Jeremy couldn't help laughing.

"Guys, can you focus for just one second!" Devon implored.

The bird was flying on and off the top of the structure covering the slide. Jeremy and Devon ducked under the opening, climbed up the stairs and sat inside the fort at the top. It was a tight space and while difficult to move around, it was clearly empty. Peering out, Jeremy spotted someone approaching from the other end of the park. The bird was also visible in an orange tree. Directly below it was a pile of fruit.

Jeremy's eyes drifted from the bird to the person who was closer now. Suddenly it dawned on Jeremy where he had seen him. He was the guy Jeremy had seen at the church and castle, the one with the stripe on his shirt. Wondering what he was doing at the park, Jeremy hurried down the slide and started to run to the tree, almost bumping into the stranger.

"Sorry," the man said. "I didn't mean to startle you."

"Then perhaps you shouldn't sneak up like that," Jeremy snapped back.

Briefly holding up a TDC badge the man said, "There's been another change in plans."

"What's with all the changes?" Devon asked, coming up next to Jeremy.

"Yeah, sorry about that. This is the last one. It's just that there's someone trying to get the stones and we need to get them out of Portugal before the wrong person gets their hands on them. Have you found them all yet?"

"You do know we just got here yesterday? You didn't expect us to be done yet, did you?" Jeremy wasn't sure why but he was getting annoyed and speaking with a bit of an attitude, his face burning.

Jeremy noticed surprise in the man's eyes but it was gone as soon as it appeared. "Of course not. But you will have to be a bit quick finding them. It's important that you meet me at Saint George's Castle at 10:00 am in three days time. Can you do that?"

"But that's only two...,"

Jeremy touched Devon's arm to stop her from saying more. She looked at him quizzically but didn't interrupt as he spoke. "Okay, we can do that." Glancing at their parents who were seated at the café, he saw his mom wave. "I think we need to get back."

"Of course," the man replied, walking back the way he'd come.

They were headed toward their parents, when Jeremy suddenly insisted, "Follow me." He climbed back up into the fort like structure, hitting his head while trying to sit down. Rubbing his new bump, he waited for Devon to join him.

"What was that about? Why did you cut me off?"

"Something isn't right. There's something about that guy. I knew what you were going to say. He wants us to meet him just two hours earlier than the woman from the TDC. Why would two hours be such a big deal? And did you notice how surprised he was when I said we'd only gotten here yesterday?"

"No."

"Well, I did, though he tried to cover it up."

Only then did Jeremy think to look at Thing and Birdbrain. They were the same: purple on Thing's feet and Birdbrain's beak. "Did you happen to see our buddies when we were standing next to him?"

"No, I was too focused on him," she said.

"Me, too."

"Wait. Why didn't I think of this sooner?" Devon consulted Birdbrain. "Is that guy dangerous? Did you change colors?"

"I don't know. I was watching the bird. Sorry."

Devon turned to Thing. "I wasn't paying attention."

"What were you ..." Jeremy started to ask Thing.

"It wouldn't matter anyways. I'm colorblind."

"Oh, you have got to be kidding!" Jeremy almost yelled. "How can you be colorblind? You were changing colors earlier just for fun?"

"I can feel…"

"Devon, Jeremy," voices called out.

"We better go where they can see us," Devon said.

They slid down the slide and went over, waving to their parents so they could see them through the trees. "Fifteen minutes and then we need to go," Devon's mom called out.

"Okay," they both yelled back.

Running back up to the top of the slide and sitting inside the structure, Jeremy was careful, this time, not to hit his head.

Devon pointed, "Hey, the bird is still up in the tree."

Sure enough, she was right. Jeremy went down the slide with Devon close behind.

"Do you see anything?" she asked.

"You mean besides lots of oranges? I see a couple of rocks but they all look the same."

"Let's hold our buddies and see if one of the rocks changes colors," Devon replied.

They held their buddies but nothing stood out. Moving oranges from the pile, some split open during their fall from the tree, they found nothing.

Thing was kicking Jeremy again.

"What."

"Will you please take me off this stupid leash?"

"Fine. You're not helping anyways."

Jeremy stood up, looking around, frustrated. "Wait. Remember the clue." Jeremy spoke from memory: "'He needs you to find the four colored objects that help him breathe.' The clue doesn't say we have to find four stones."

Stepping back, his eyes rose from the ground to scan the tree. Devon must have done the same because she said, "What's Thing doing up in the tree?"

"According to him, not being helpful," Thing replied, kicking something out from a crook in the tree.

Falling to the ground was a flat, brown object. Jeremy went to pick it up when Thing said, "No, that's for Devon, not you."

Devon stepped forward and picked up a cold, round piece of metal. "It looks like a medallion." She grabbed Birdbrain in her other hand and the brown piece glowed red.

Hearing their parents' voices again Devon turned away from the tree, putting the medallion in her pocket.

"Are you coming?" Jeremy asked Thing.

"Not until you apologize."

"Okay, you're right. You have been helpful. I'm sorry."

"Thank you."

And with that Thing jumped down from the tree and into Jeremy's hand. Jeremy looked up at the church on the hill and thought he saw a tall, dark figure looking down. A cold shiver ran through his body.

11. Devon Opens Up

Jeremy's mind was racing as they walked back to the tram stop and rode back to their apartments.

"You have that lost in space look on your face again," Devon remarked.

Only then did he realize they had made it back. "Mom," he called out, "can Devon and I hang out here for a bit? We won't go anywhere."

"Sure," she said.

Devon turned to her parents. "Yeah, that's fine," her dad said. "Twenty minutes, okay? We need to get ready for dinner."

"Thanks Dad."

Once they were settled down on the curb, Jeremy spoke first. "We're missing something."

"And that's new?" Thing remarked. Devon smiled.

"Be glad Birdbrain's so quiet," Jeremy said as he glared down at Thing who started pretending to do the breaststroke while hooked to the side of Jeremy's jeans.

"Well," Devon said, chuckling but turning serious as she twirled her hair, "I think it's a bit odd there are two people from the TDC asking us to bring them stones two hours apart, and they would say stones when it seems that's not what we were asked to find."

"Actually, the woman said objects and the man said stones. Jeremy's gaze fixed on Devon's hand as she wrapped her hair around her fingers. "And did you actually see their badges?" he asked.

"Well, no," she said. "They flashed them pretty quickly."

Jeremy's mind started racing. TDC, TDC. "Unclip Birdbrain," he told Devon as he did the same to Thing. They put them side-by-side. "Look at their TDC stamps."

"Beautiful, right?" Thing interrupted.

"They're the same, so." Devon appeared to be trying hard to ignore Thing but he had switched from breast to butterfly stroke and making it difficult.

"So, the man's from the park was different."

"How do you -" Devon started but Jeremy cut her off.

"See here," he pointed, "where ours have a blue background with yellow letters and red trim all around?" Not waiting for an answer, he continued, "the man's had purple trim and a red background."

Devon stared at him.

"Remember," Jeremy sighed, "when we were at Saint George's Castle and I could remember odd things about it?"

She nodded.

"Well, I have a really, really good memory. I'm not sure how or why but I can remember things I've seen easily. And I can promise you, his badge was different."

She looked at him a minute. "Okay. But what does that mean."

"I'm not sure. Perhaps he's lying. But then who is he?"

Something else started nagging Jeremy. He was hesitant to mention anything but Devon said, "What?"

He stood up and began pacing. Thing switched to the back stroke. "I have this weird feeling we were put together for a reason. But I'm not sure why. How did they pair us up? Heck, why would the TDC want us to work together? Do we have something in common, or…?"

"Maybe they thought Birdbrain and I would make a good team," Thing interjected.

"Yeah, you're right," Birdbrain added, causing everyone to stop and look at her as she had been quiet and still at Devon's side.

Regarding Birdbrain with curiosity for a moment, Devon turned back to Jeremy. "Well I heard my dad say that he and your mom work at the same company and they'd met before at a conference."

Jeremy stopped pacing. "Oh, okay. Maybe that's it."

"And ..." Devon paused, gazing down at her feet.

"What? Do you have an idea?" Jeremy sat back down beside her. "We could really use some help right about now."

"It's just that I usually don't tell people but it seems silly not to tell you."

"What?" He stared at her, waiting.

She met his gaze. "I'm adopted too."

Incredulous, a second passed before he responded. "Wait, what! Wow, you're right, I never would have guessed that. You look so much like your parents."

Devon had unclipped Birdbrain and was turning her over in her hands. "That's what people say but I don't really, if you look closely. Our skin color is the same and I think people just make assumptions, which works for me. I don't get any questions … unlike you, I'm sure."

"Yeah. Lots of questions and stares and sometimes rude comments." Jeremy's eyes gazed at the buildings across the street without seeing them.

They were both silent for a moment. Jeremy turned to face Devon. "We have that in common but so what?"

"Well…okay. So, people assume I'm not adopted because I look similar to my parents. And it sounds like people assume that you and your mom aren't a family because you don't have the same skin color, right?"

"Yeah, so."

"This adoption thing," Thing interrupted, "is that why you and your mom don't match? You never did answer my question."

"Yes, Thing," Jeremy said as he glanced down at Thing and then back to Devon as she continued.

"So maybe we were put together because they needed a team that wouldn't make assumptions. And perhaps the man in the park wants us to assume he's with the TDC."

"Uh huh."

She thought about it some more. "Well, it's possible. And maybe if we weren't careful we would assume the man was from the TDC because he flashed a badge at us, but maybe his badge is fake."

Now Jeremy continued, "And that might explain why he asked us to find stones. Maybe he's just guessing what we're looking for because he doesn't actually know and since we found a stone first, he assumed we had to find more." He chuckled. "It seems like we're all getting into trouble by making assumptions."

12. Empty Clue

Jeremy and his mom went to Devon's apartment the next morning for breakfast. Jeremy really wanted to go to the science museum with Devon so when Devon's dad asked, "Why doesn't Jeremy come with us?" he gave his mom the sweetest smile he could muster. "You can take the day for yourself," Devon's dad suggested.

"I appreciate that but I'd like to spend the day with Jeremy." Jeremy's shoulders sagged as his mom continued. "I have a place I want to show him and then maybe we'll head to the museum later." Jeremy started to protest but she cut him off. "We're all going to Sintra together tomorrow. You can see Devon then."

Jeremy heard the finality in her voice and knew better than to argue. Biting his tongue, he turned to Devon.

"Hey, I want to show you something," Devon said. "Follow me." She got up from the table and headed toward her room.

"Clear the table first, please," her dad said.

Jeremy and Devon hurriedly took the plates off the table and placed them on the kitchen counter then went into Devon's room.

"Do you think the third thing is at the museum?" Jeremy wondered as they entered Devon's room.

"Thing! You're looking for another thing? I knew it. I knew you didn't think much of me but to equate me with a rock is insulting!" And with a kick to Jeremy's leg, Thing turned his back.

Jeremy stopped and stared at Devon, silently asking for help but she just shrugged her shoulders.

"You're right, I'm sorry. And you are way cooler than a rock."

Thing didn't respond.

Jeremy turned back to Devon. "I guess we each have to look for whatever it is on our own."

"What are we supposed to do with these… objects anyways?" Devon asked.

"I'm not sure but you have a bird that doesn't like to talk much and my buddy is now giving me the silent treatment so not sure if they'll be of much help," Jeremy replied.

***

Jeremy and his mom spent the morning at Elevador de Santa Justa. Climbing nearly 150 feet, it raised them up the equivalent of seven stories from which they had an excellent view of the city. While initially grumpy because he couldn't hang with Devon, he was soon distracted by the sights and history, including the fact that the elevator was built by an apprentice of Gustave Eiffel, the architect of the Eiffel tower in Paris.

"Can we go to the Eiffel Tower someday, Mom?" Jeremy asked.

"That would be fun, wouldn't it?" she smiled.

Thing was uncharacteristically silent the entire time and ignored all of Jeremy's attempts at interaction. Jeremy finally gave up.

After lunch, his mom asked, "Would you still like to go to the museum?"

"Yeah. It's supposed to be interesting. At least that's what Devon said." After taking the train and walking for ten minutes, they found it. Once inside the museum there were a bunch of exhibits that reminded Jeremy of the Exploratorium in San Francisco: Displays exploring light and sound, mirrors that distorted people's reflections, exhibits that demonstrated the laws of physics. As they went around he kept looking at Thing who just hung on the side of his jeans though occasionally Jeremy caught him glaring up at him.

"Are you still mad at me? I apologized you know." But Thing just closed his eyes.

After passing a boy riding a bicycle across a rope suspended two floors high, they entered a room with a mini two-story construction site complete with a crane and carts on tracks.

Jeremy stood watching kids play and wished he was young enough to join in and not look silly. He was about to leave when he noticed that Thing was blue.

"Mom, do you mind if I spend a little time here?"

"If you want. I'll go get a cup of coffee and meet you back up here. Just don't go anywhere else, okay?" she said.

Jeremy wandered around, ducking to walk under the house and climbing stairs to the second floor. He even searched the guard shack from which one could control a crossing gate with a stop sign, looking for anything that might be one of the missing objects but there was nothing. A couple of times Jeremy stopped to help the younger kids when they were trying to put big red and blue blocks into the metal house frame to form the walls.

His mom came back and waved to him. Feeling defeated, he walked out of the area and saw Thing turn orange. "You're supposed to help me, you know. Why didn't you tell me when we were close to another …object?" Jeremy asked Thing. But Thing still had his eyes closed and didn't respond.

13. Statues And Castles

The next morning, both families walked to catch the train that would take them to Sintra. Jeremy and Devon again intentionally trailed a short distance behind. "Did you have any luck at the museum?" Jeremy asked.

"No. Birdbrain turned blue once but I couldn't figure out why. Did you?"

"Did Birdbrain change colors around that construction site?"

"Yeah. I went in and looked around but didn't find anything."

"Me too."

"How did we miss it?" Devon asked, exasperation in her voice. "I know Thing is mad at you but Birdbrain would have told me if she'd seen something."

"I know." Jeremy closed his eyes in frustration. "How can this work out now?" He unzipped his jacket, the day already warmer than expected.

"If we do find what we need are you okay meeting the lady from the TDC by yourself?" Devon asked.

"Sure. But that's a big if, isn't it? Plus, since you'll be on a plane back home we don't have much choice." He crinkled his nose as he passed men smoking on the sidewalk. Turning a corner, Jeremy and Devon saw the statue of the horse and rider towering over the square.

"Mom, can Devon and I run over and take a look at the statue real quick?" Jeremy asked.

"Sure," she said. "But hurry so we don't miss our train."

Devon and Jeremy ran over to the statue that was atop a tall white marble base 30 feet high. Carved in the sides were a face and the words "King John I." The rider sat erect, a long spear in one hand, wearing a helmet adorned with a large feather. To Jeremy the horse looked mighty proud and appeared to be prancing. The base of the statue was smooth except for a few dents in the side.

"Jeremy, Devon! Come on!" his mom called. Jeremy ran his hands over the side of the base, in and out of the holes as he passed.

They left the statue and rejoined their parents. Crossing the street to the train station, he gazed up to see carved figures standing along every part of the building, which was made of white stone. "We don't have anything like this back home," he said out loud to no one in particular.

"Who are you talking to? You aren't going cuckoo, are you?"

Jeremy glared down at Thing.

"Well, are you?"

"Shush."

"Don't shush me," Thing said as he started pushing off from the side of Jeremy's leg only to be stopped by the carabiner clip.

"Will you stop!"

"Everything okay back there, Jeremy?" his mom called over her shoulder.

"Yeah, fine."

Coming up next to him, Devon was trying hard not to laugh.

"Really, how did I get so lucky?" Jeremy asked sarcastically.

"Oh, I think you two are perfect for each other," Devon chuckled.

Jeremy started to glare at her but then started chuckling.

"Well, at least he's talking to you again," she smiled.

"Did you see anything when you looked at the statue?" Devon asked once they were seated on the train.

"No," Jeremy replied, "just some holes. Did you find anything?"

"Same as you," she replied.

Forty-five minutes later they arrived in Sintra and made their way to the #48 bus. It took another twenty minutes to reach their first stop, the Castle of the Moors. They had to walk a ways down a path but it was shaded and cool. They finally reached the gate and after showing their tickets, wandered in.

"Whoa," Jeremy uttered under his breath. "This is amazing."

"Who are you-?"

"Cut it, Thing."

Jeremy took in the scene in front of him. Stone steps rose to the left and right along stone walls with battlements placed at intervals. The steps seemed endless. He raced ahead and started going up the stairs on the left.

"Please walk," his mom called out.

"Okay," he said, not really slowing down.

Racing up to a battlement, Jeremy could see over all of Sintra and beyond. He found the train station and other buildings they had driven past. He realized the small town was surrounded by dense forest. To his left, the narrow steps went up and up and up. To the right, it was the same.

"Jeremy," Devon called out. "Wait for me."

Catching up to him, they continued at a slower pace, climbing the stairs and turning off to look over walls along the way. As they got higher he saw something in the distance.

"Can we go back down please?"

Jeremy looked over at Devon. "Did you say something?"

"No."

"Can we go back down, please?" It was Birdbrain.

"Is something wrong?" Devon asked, peering down at her side.

"Um, no. I'd just rather…I don't like…" Birdbrain was having a hard time finishing a sentence.

Jeremy started laughing. "I think you have a bird that is afraid of heights."

Devon appeared to be having difficulty deciding whether to be angry with Jeremy for laughing, or laugh herself.

"Why don't you close your eyes?" Devon suggested.

Birdbrain squeezed her eyes tight. After a moment, she started shaking and opened them again. "Oh, it's no use. I'm a failure. I'm a terrible magic buddy. Leave it to me to be the only bird afraid of heights."

Devon tried to console her. "You're just fine, Birdbrain. We all have things we're scared of."

"Like what?"

"Um, spiders. I don't like spiders. Jeremy?"

"I'm not afraid-." The plea for help in Devon's eyes made him stop. "Lost. Getting lost."

"See, it happens to all of us."

"Not me." Thing said. "I'm not afraid of anything."

"Oh really," Jeremy said, reaching as if to squeeze Thing to turn him off. His hand paused in midair. "That's it!" He turned to Devon. "Why don't you just turn Birdbrain off for a bit?"

"What do you think, Birdbrain?" Devon asked, looking down at her buddy. "Are you okay with that?"

Birdbrain nodded. Devon took Birdbrain in her hand and squeezed gently, and the bird closed her eyes. They continued up the steps, then heard, "It didn't work. I'm still here. Oh no, what am I going to do?"

"Let me try again," Devon said. She did and nothing happened.

Jeremy heard a snicker, which turned into laughter. "What?" he asked, peering down at Thing.

"You. Can't. Turn. Me. Off. Hah!"

"Why don't I put her in my backpack?" Jeremy suggested, trying to ignore Thing who was jumping, repeatedly, off his leg, still laughing.

Devon glanced at Birdbrain who nodded her head, and placed her in his pack. "Thing. You really need to stop before someone notices," Devon scolded.

Thing stopped jumping, but his eyes sparkled and he continued to laugh as he caught Jeremy's eye.

Jeremy did his best to stifle a laugh as it was all quite funny.

14. What Is Lost

They continued up the stairs and after several more minutes
Jeremy recognized the object in the distance. "Look, Devon," he
said, "another castle. But wait, there's something odd about it. It's
all gray. Isn't that the one that's painted all crazy?"

"Do you still have that brochure on Sintra and the castles?" she
asked.

"Yeah."

"Let me see it."

He took it out of his pack. The Moorish Castle was pictured on
the front. On the back was the castle in the distance: The National
Palace of Pena. In the brochure, it was full of all these amazing,

bright colors; mustard yellow, red, peach, light bluish/purple. In front of them it was dull and gray.

"What happened to the palace?" Jeremy wondered aloud.

Moments later their parents came up behind them. "I heard about it on the news," his mom said. "One morning, about three weeks ago, the sun came up and the castle had mysteriously lost all of its colors. News reports suggested a group of vandals came and painted over it one night."

"We have to get to that castle," Jeremy said to Devon under his breath. "Something valuable has disappeared."

"I think you're right," she said quietly. They had turned their back to their parents, pretending to look out over the stone walls to the trees below. "I was thinking that something valuable meant an object but maybe not. And the objects we have found so far are colored."

"Let's go check out that castle!" Jeremy exclaimed, turning quickly to go back down the steps.

"Wait, Jeremy," his mom said. "We still have the entire other side of this castle to visit."

His disappointment must have shown on his face, because Devon pulled him aside. "Remember the riddle. We need to find four objects. How do we know we won't find one of them here?"

Realizing she was right, he perked up and gave her a smile. "Okay, let's keep looking," he said.

Forty-five minutes and one snack later, Devon and Jeremy were stumped and tired. As they were back down at the base of the stairs, Devon had taken Birdbrain out of Jeremy's backpack and she was now next to them on the bench.

In a flash, Birdbrain was gone, carried away by a real bird who had snatched her up without warning.

"Hey!" Devon cried out.

Jeremy caught a flash of yellow amongst the light blue feathers.

"Devon, it's the same bird!" He jumped to his feet. "We'll be right back Mom!"

They ran up thirty stairs until they reached Birdbrain, who was sitting on a battlement wall shaking with her eyes closed. She was blue. The real bird was nowhere in sight.

Devon grabbed a shaking Birdbrain and clipped her back on to her belt loop. They searched the area but found nothing. "Now what?" Jeremy wondered if they'd gone crazy, following a bird around a castle.

"Over there." Thing called up to Jeremy from where he was clipped to the side of his jeans.

"Where?" Jeremy asked.

"Over there."

"Where is over there?"

"Oh, will you just unclip me!"

Exasperated, Jeremy did just that, placing Thing on the ground.

Thing waddled over to a wall of the battlement and pointed between two stones that were low to the ground.

On his hands and knees, Jeremy peered between the stones and pulled out a white, round piece of metal. He handed it to Devon who grabbed Birdbrain and the metal turned a mustard yellow color.

"We found it!" he exclaimed.

"Ahem."

Smiling, Jeremy said, "I know, I know. You found it, Thing."

"And…"

"And thank you."

"You're welcome."

"You know, I must admit Thing. You're pretty awesome."

"I know," Thing said, as he back flipped onto Jeremy's foot.

Laughing, they walked back down the stairs to their parents who were waiting below. "Mom, is it lunchtime?" Jeremy asked.

"With you it's always lunchtime." She smiled.

They sat and ate a lunch of turkey sandwiches, apples and chocolate chip cookies. As they got ready to leave, Jeremy asked, "Mom, is there anything else?"

"Here," she said. "Catch." She threw him an apple. He ate it as they headed off for the bus and the mysterious palace.

15. Assumptions

Jeremy and Devon intentionally hung back from their parents as they walked toward the bus. "So, we've found two medallions and one rock," Jeremy said. "I wonder what the fourth object is."

"Maybe there's a pattern," Devon suggested.

"Like what?"

Devon was quiet for a moment before she answered. "Well, two of the things are similar in that they're both medallions, only different colors."

"So?"

"So, it's just an observation."

"Two of them almost match." Jeremy thought out loud. "Both are metal, unlike the stone. But they don't quite match because they're different colors."

"Like you and your mom," Thing chimed in.

"What?"

"You and your mom. Your brown and she's cream but you're both people. Though I still don't get why you don't match. Oh wait, you're adopted, right."

"Okay. But that still doesn't answer the question of what we need to find."

"Do I really have to spell it out for you?" Thing asked.

Jeremy stopped and looked down at him. "What am I missing now?"

"You and your mom are the same but different, right?"

"I think that's been established, Thing."

"Well, Devon and her parents are more similar." Thing paused a moment and then turned to Devon. "Please tell me you're following what I'm saying, 'cause he obviously isn't."

"You're suggesting we need to find a stone that looks like the one we already have," she said.

"Really, I don't know what you'd do without me," Thing stated, while doing yet another backflip off Jeremy's leg.

"I know," Jeremy replied. Seeing doubt in Thing's eyes he continued with more enthusiasm, "No, really, Thing. I do."

Back on the bus, Devon and Jeremy were both quietly staring out the window. At the entrance to Pena Palace, people were bustling about talking excitedly. Pieces of conversations floated in the air.

"No color…"

"How did it happen…?"

"It seems like magic."

They took the long uphill path toward the castle, staying a bit ahead of their parents. Jeremy told Devon what had been bugging him on the short bus ride. "Why are we assuming the tall, dark man is somehow bad?" Picking up a rock, he turned it over in his hands and then threw it in some bushes. "I mean, I know the lady told us not to talk to him but why are we believing her, besides the fact that she looked nice?"

"She had a TDC badge, remember."

"True. But what if the man did too? We never gave him a chance to show us one."

"I guess he looks like he could be the bad guy and she looks so sweet," Devon said.

Jeremy stopped midstep. "I'm gonna be that guy one day."

Red flashed on Devon's face and she looked down to the ground, avoiding Jeremy's gaze. After a moment, she raised her head. "Sorry."

"It's okay." He broke eye contact and peered off into the distance. "The crazy thing is, I was thinking the same thing." They continued walking before a thought occurred to him. "I didn't see her badge, did you? She flashed it even quicker than the man at the park. He stopped and turned to face Devon. "Remember when we talked about how everyone assumes who we are, who are families are? We're still assuming things ourselves based on how people look. It's clouding our judgment. Perhaps we were put together because someone expected us to see things differently."

"Our buddies have been a bit purple since we talked to her," Devon's voice trailed off.

As they continued, the castle came into view, appearing gray and cold. Jeremy held the pamphlet advertising tours of the castle and the difference was amazing. "Let's hope we find the rock here because after this we're going our separate ways."

"Don't remind me," Devon responded. Jeremy glanced at her and she continued. "I like traveling with you, is all."

Jeremy smiled as they went inside. Ten minutes later, after being stuck behind yet another line of people as they slowly snaked through a room decorated with furniture from 18 grew antsy.

"Mom, can I go outside? I'm a bit bored."

"Sure, but stay close by."

Devon continued with her parents, leaving him to explore the outside of the castle on his own.

He wandered outside, glad to be alone, thinking of the conversation Devon and he had on the walk up to the castle. Lost in thought and not paying attention to his surroundings, he bumped into someone.

16. The Man From The TDC

"Are you going to run away again, Jeremy?" It was the man he and Devon had just been discussing. He addressed Jeremy with a twinkle in his eye.

Jeremy took a step back.

"Psst." It was Thing. He was back to his old self. His feet, purple since Saint George's Castle, were orange again.

"No, not this time. But hey, how do you know my name?"

"I was there when you were picked for the club. I sent you your buddy."

"Do you know what he named me?" Thing asked.

"Not now," Jeremy said. Addressing the man he asked, "You're the one behind the Travelers Detective Club?"

"I'm one of them. You could consider me second in command."

"Thing! He named me Thing!" Thing started bouncing off Jeremy's leg and Jeremy reached down to hold him still.

The man chuckled but kept his gaze on Jeremy.

"I'm sorry we ran away," Jeremy said.

"Unfortunately, I get that quite a bit. But I was expecting that if anyone wouldn't, it would be you."

Jeremy saw kindness in his eyes but also an intensity that caused him to look away. "I know. I'm a bit frustrated with myself." After a brief pause he turned back to the man. "Who's the other one, the woman who talked to us the other day?"

"She's part of a group that likes to take the smaller joys out of life. We heard she wants the stones and medallions to get rid of more color from the world. Rumor has it she wants to steal the red from the Golden Gate Bridge next. We knew she was going to come and try to take them from you, so here I am."

"Why didn't she just get them herself?"

"She doesn't know what to look for. Not having a magic buddy, she needs you to find them."

"You know there's another guy following us." Jeremy looked around as he said this.

The man kept his eyes on Jeremy. "Yes, that was rather unexpected. I'm not sure who he is."

"So, what now?"

"If I'm correct you have one more stone to find, yes?"

Jeremy nodded. "So, it is a stone."

"Yes, it is."

"If you can find it today, go to the horseman tonight."

"Why can't you just get it?" Jeremy asked.

"Because I am an adult. The magic buddies won't work, even with me."

There was a muffled sound from Thing who was still being held by Jeremy. "What?" Jeremy asked, as he let go of him.

"If you keep doing that I won't work with you either!"

Jeremy turned back to the man. "What if the others try to stop us?"

"I will be shadowing you and will do my best to keep them away. However, I can't promise I can stop them."

"What do you mean you can't stop them? Aren't you supposed to be able to do magic? You gave me my magic buddy, remember."

He looked at Jeremy with a kind expression. "I cannot do magic, only your buddies can. But if we use our brains that will be enough."

Jeremy was beginning to be doubtful that they were going to be able to finish what they started.

Placing his hand on Jeremy's shoulder he said, "Jeremy, trust me. No. Trust yourself. You can do this." He peered over his shoulder before continuing. "Here's what I was thinking: Get decoys to give to the woman, should she approach you."

"I could just kick her," Thing suggested.

"Then after she leaves," the man continued, "pull out the real ones."

"That seems a little too simple. Do you really think she'll fall for it?" Jeremy asked.

"We can hope. Of course, if you have another idea, do what feels right."

"Okay," Jeremy said, not at all feeling okay. "Oops." He looked down the stairs and saw Devon and their parents come out of the castle. "I have to go."

The man nodded and strode away as Jeremy turned and went down the stairs.

"Hey Mom, can Devon and I wander around the outside a bit longer?"

"It's getting late Jeremy. I'd like to get back."

"Please. Just a little longer. Can we have fifteen minutes?"

His mom sighed.

"Your mom's right. It's getting late," Devon's mom said.

Worried, Jeremy looked at Devon. They hung back from their parents and walked as slow as they dared on the way back to the bus. He filled her in on what had happened while she was inside the castle. Devon stopped and turned toward the castle above.

"The bird! It's right there!" Devon pointed back toward the castle, where the blue bird with yellow tail feathers perched in a tree.

Devon and Jeremy turned to each other and at the same time said, "Bathroom!"

Devon yelled down at her parents, "Mom, Dad, I have to go to the bathroom. I'll be right back."

"Me too," Jeremy added and they both turned and ran up the hill without waiting for a response.

Racing to the tree where the bird sat, they peered under the tree only to find multiple stones. They started grabbing them, while holding their buddies. Jeremy put the first two stones in his pocket but continued searching through the pile.

"I found it!" Devon cried out, handing a stone to Jeremy.

Before he could look at it, a voice behind him said, "Why don't you give it to me now?" Turning around slowly, while at the same time putting the rock in his pocket, Jeremy came face to face with the woman pretending to be from the TDC. With a smile on her face, she added, "That way you don't have to meet me tomorrow."

Panic rose in Jeremy and he turned to Devon who said, "But we left the other objects in our room. Don't you want them all at the same time?"

"No, why don't you give me what you have now and I'll get the rest tomorrow."

Reaching into his pocket Jeremy felt for one of the stones he had picked up earlier and handed it to her. He then said, "We have to go." He grabbed Devon's hand and pulled her away and they ran back down the hill. They didn't stop until they caught up with their parents. Jeremy's heart was still pounding as the bus pulled away and headed back to the train station.

17. Putting It Together

Later that day, as Devon and Jeremy walked down to a store near their apartments, she asked, "I wonder what we're supposed to do with the things we found? All along we've been focused on finding them, but how are they supposed to help the horseman breathe? Does he really come alive? And what happens if he does?"

"Let's go back to the riddle," Jeremy suggested. "Something valuable has disappeared. Only the horseman can bring it back. He needs you to find the four colored objects that help him breathe. Castles, museums and playgrounds will give you what you need to complete this task."

"Okay, you do have a good memory," Thing said.

Jeremy smiled down at Thing who was bouncing slightly at the side of Jeremy's pants.

"We found four colored objects that are the same colors lost from the castle walls. And we found them at castles and a playground. But what about the museum?" Devon wondered. "What did the museum give us? Neither of us found anything there."

"I know. But our buddies did change color," Jeremy replied.

"We did?" asked Thing.

"Yes," Jeremy said. "You were mad at me and had your eyes closed a lot but you changed colors when we were at the construction site." They continued down the sidewalk, waiting for a gray truck to pass before crossing a one-way street. "Oh, how did we miss it?" Jeremy exclaimed, stopping and turning to face Devon, causing a man walking close behind to have to stop suddenly to avoid bumping into them. The stranger passed by, muttering in Portuguese, and Jeremy called out "Sorry," before turning back to Devon. "Thing never turned yellow when I left," he said. "Did Birdbrain?"

"Now that you mention it, I don't think she did."

"Remember," Jeremy continued, "if we're close to a clue but walk away they turn yellow but Thing went right back to orange."

He glanced at Thing who was climbing up his pant leg as high as the carabiner clip would allow and then letting go and dropping back down. Looking up, he continued, "What did we do besides search for an object?"

"I didn't do anything else, did you?" Devon asked.

"I helped kids put foam blocks into the house frame," Jeremy answered. "At times they were too big for the little kids to handle and they needed my help to push them in just right."

"Huh," Devon replied. She looked down at Birdbrain whose eyes were open but was just hanging at her side. "Wait, that's it!" Devon almost shouted, causing Birdbrain to flap her wings and peer up at her. Devon turned back to Jeremy. "Remember the holes in the base of the statue? Perhaps we place them there! Let's run over and check the statue. It's only a few blocks away."

"Wow. You can actually get excited about something," he said smiling.

"Stop," Devon said, pushing Jeremy playfully on the shoulder.

"First let's buy what we need at the tourist shop," he said. "We're almost there." Grabbing two silver colored medallions from one of the multitude of trinket-filled buckets lining the doorway, they paid and left.

They ran all the way to the statue, not stopping until they reached the square. While catching their breath, they walked up to and around the statue. "I see two indentations!" Devon cried out.

"Me too!" Jeremy replied. "The rocks will fit on this side."

"The medallions will fit here," Devon said. "What now, though?" she continued. "We can't just walk up to the statue in the middle of the day and hopefully help the horseman breathe, whatever that means, with everyone watching."

"We need to come back tonight, remember. That's what the man from the TDC said to do," Jeremy replied. "We'll sneak out after everyone is asleep and come back with our things. There's bound to be fewer people around."

"Oh, you're going to get in so much trouble," Thing exclaimed as he bounced a backflip off Jeremy's leg.

Devon stopped. "Sneak out? Are you serious?"

"Do you have a better idea?" Jeremy said as he turned to face her. "Look, I know it's risky, but if we want to follow this through what choice do we have?"

Birdbrain chimed in. "He's right, you know."

18. Close Call

While his mom was in the bathroom later that night, Jeremy placed a folded piece of paper in the door jam.

"You're really going to do this, aren't you?" Thing asked.

"We have to, Thing."

"What happens if your mom finds out?"

"I don't want to think about it. Let's just hope she doesn't."

Lying in bed that night, the room was dark except for a sliver of light from the street. Jeremy forced his eyes to stay open. It wasn't hard as Thing kept kicking him in the side.

He met Devon outside on the street near her apartment. "Did you have any trouble getting out?"

"No. But if they catch me gone I'm done."

"I know what you mean. Ready?" he asked.

"Ready."

It took them only three to four minutes to reach the statue. Once there they searched for the holes again, using flashlights they had stashed in their pockets. "What do we do?" Jeremy asked. "Just put them in?"

"I guess so," Devon replied, a hint of doubt in her voice.

Jeremy had the mustard yellow and red colored medallions that were now cold and colorless. Devon had the blue and peach colored stones, now gray, the last one she had found at the palace. They each put their objects in their respective places and stood back. Nothing happened. They waited a bit longer but the statue didn't change.

"You're kidding me!" Jeremy cried, unable to contain his frustration. "We've done all this for nothing? What the…"

"Breathe Jeremy," Devon implored. "Let's think for a minute."

"Watch out!" Thing shouted from Jeremy's side.

Spinning around, he bumped into the lady pretending to be from the TDC, and dropped his flashlight.

As he stood facing her in the dark, there was enough light from distant streetlights to see her face. Her eyes glared with a malice that took his breath away. A wicked grin that made him think of an evil witch made the hairs on the back of his neck stand straight up.

"So, you tried to trick me! The stone you gave me must be a fake after all. Give me the right ones! You don't want to double cross me again!" She grabbed his left arm and held her other hand open, palm up. He wrenched his arm away, reached into his pocket and dropped two stones on the ground. The clattering of the medallions Devon dropped on the other side of the statue drew the woman's attention and Jeremy took the moment to run away.

Jeremy and Devon both ran, not stopping until they rounded a corner and were out of sight. They peeked back around the corner. The woman was quickly walking away.

"What do we do now?" Jeremy said to Devon as he continued to watch the woman until she turned a corner out of sight. "Our plan didn't work."

"Your plan didn't work, yet." Thing said from Jeremy's side. "Don't give up now."

Jeremy was silent for a moment as he studied Thing. "Wait a second," Jeremy said as he spun around toward Devon. "When the smaller kids at the museum had really big foam pieces to put in place they needed help and we had to make sure to push the pieces in at the same time or it wouldn't work."

Picking up where his voice trailed off Devon continued, "Maybe we have to place them into the statue at the same time."

"How do we know when it's safe to come out?" Devon asked.

"I'm not sure." As Jeremy spoke, the man from the TDC stepped out from behind a building, and standing under a streetlight, waved his hand. "It must be okay."

Running back to the statue they grabbed the rocks and medallions out of the statue. "Okay, on the count of three," Jeremy said.

"One...two...three." He took the medallions and placed them in the holes while Devon did the same with the rocks. It was quiet except for an occasional car driving by. Jeremy looked at the rocks, wondering if the lady was going to come back or if their plan was going to work, when they started to glow.

Soon the entire horse was glowing in a swirl of yellow, peach, blue and red. Jeremy scurried to his feet and backed away, almost bumping into Devon who was doing the same. Before their eyes, the colors rose through the horse's legs, its body, and up through the rider. The colors swirled around as if a strong wind was blowing them, and then they disappeared. Jeremy held his breath, wondering what would happen next when he saw a flick of the horse's tail and a turn of the horseman's head. The horseman beckoned to them. "Well, come on. Climb up. You are coming with me, aren't you?"

19. A Flight To Remember

Jeremy glanced at Devon who had a big smile on her face as she shrugged and reached for the horseman's hand. As Jeremy followed, Devon cried, "Hurry!"

Peering over his shoulder, he saw the man from the park running toward them. In their excitement both Jeremy and Devon had completely forgotten about him. As Jeremy jumped on, the horseman nudged his steed with his foot, and it started galloping. The horse's hooves left the pavement as they rose off the ground. Jeremy felt a rush of wind on his face.

"No, no, no, no, nooooooo." Birdbrain had buried her head in Devon's side.

"I'm sorry, Birdbrain. But we can't get off," Devon said.

The stuffed bird started to cry as they climbed up into the sky, circling over and over, climbing above Lisbon. Breaking through the clouds, the moon was full and bright, lighting their way. Jeremy felt Devon's grip on his waist lighten as he, in turn, relaxed his hold on the horseman.

"This is awesome!" Thing cried out. "Oh, come on Birdbrain. Just open your eyes."

"No, I can't."

"The moon is amazing and the clouds are so soft."

Birdbrain pulled herself away from Devon's back and peeked at the night sky.

"Oh wow! You're right."

"Nice job, buddy," Jeremy whispered to Thing.

As the horseman started to descend, slowly circling the sky, Devon suggested, "Birdbrain, you might want to close your eyes now."

"No. I want to see what happens."

Coming down from the clouds, the darkness was striking, but as their eyes adjusted, the outline of the Moorish Castle and then Pena Palace came into view.

The horseman pointed his long, thin spear at the palace as they came closer. They circled it over and over as the horseman kept the spear aimed at the towering structure. There was a flash of light, and for a moment, the palace was lit up as if it was the middle of a sunny day. Brilliant colors marked the walls: mustard yellow, red, peach and light bluish purple.

Jeremy felt Devon hug him tighter and glancing back he saw a big smile on her face.

"We did it!" Thing exclaimed, catching air as he did a backflip off Jeremy's side.

"This is amazing!" Birdbrain cried out.

"Isn't it beautiful?" Devon replied.

"No, not that," Birdbrain laughed. "I mean, yes, it's beautiful, but I'm not afraid anymore! I'm not afraid to be up here! Weeeeeeeeeeeeee!"

"That's great, Birdbrain." Addressing the horseman, Devon asked, "How did...I mean why did the palace lose its colors?"

"How and why. Those are good questions," he replied. "There are some out in the world who wish to take away the joy and fun in life…and the magic. Magic seems to scare some people."

"Magic?" Jeremy asked.

"How can you question magic?" Birdbrain interrupted. "Look at me. Look at Thing! La la, la la." Birdbrain let go of Devon's side and, still clipped on, flew at her side.

"Jeremy's always been a little slow," chimed in Thing. "That a way, Birdbrain!"

"There is magic everywhere," the horseman replied, smiling at the buddies. "Sometimes it shows up in grand ways as you saw tonight. And sometimes it appears in much smaller ways. You just have to look for it."

"Like the moon above the clouds," Devon said.

"I'm not afraid! I'm not afraid!" Birdbrain called out, as she continued to fly.

"Or traveling to new places and seeing new things," Jeremy added.

"Or finding a new friend when you least expect it," Devon said, smiling at Jeremy.

"I'm not afraid! I'm not afraid!"

The horseman chuckled before continuing. "As to how the palace lost its colors, I do not know. That is a question for someone else."

"I'm not afraid! I'm not-,"

"Birdbrain! Stop!" Devon cried out.

"PLUFFFFFFFF!"

"What was that?" she asked.

"Would you like to tell her?" Jeremy chuckled, glancing at Thing.

"That," Thing said, after another backflip, "was the sound of Birdbrain sticking her tongue out at you if she had a tongue, or a mouth."

All too soon they were back on the ground, the horseman helping them down from his steed. Jeremy patted the horse's head and shook the horseman's hand. "What now?" he asked.

"Turn the pieces clockwise, one at a time," the horseman replied. "Then go back to your parents. Your job here is done."

"I want to go up again!" Birdbrain cried.

"What will happen to you?" Devon asked, trying to ignore Birdbrain.

"Oh, don't worry about me," he said. "I have been given a great gift. It is not often a statue gets to come alive." With that, he gave a nod of his head and the horse flicked her tail.

"I want to go up again!"

"Birdbrain, shush!"

Devon and Jeremy reached down and one at a time turned the pieces clockwise. As they stood back, a faint glow emitted from the statue as the rocks and medallions receded into the marble base and the horseman and his horse turned back into stone.

"Noooo! I want to fly again!"

"What's gotten into you, Birdbrain?" Devon asked.

"Do you have any idea what it's like to be a magic bird that's afraid to fly? It's embarrassing! It made me want to hide. But I'm not afraid anymore. Yaaaaaaaaaaaaaay!"

"So much for having a quiet magic buddy," Jeremy laughed.

The man from the TDC was waiting for them in the shadows. "Thank you for finishing this journey even though it proved more challenging than you initially thought."

Devon and Jeremy both smiled. "Excuse me, but what's your name?" Devon asked.

He smiled. "Travis. My name is Travis." With that he turned and strode away. They watched until he was out of sight.

20. Devon Has Her Hands Full

Walking back to their street, Jeremy and Devon didn't talk, each of them lost in their own thoughts. Birdbrain, however, flapped her wings the entire walk back. "Oh, now you're fun to be with. Just when you're leaving," Thing called out.

Jeremy gave Devon a hug and patted Birdbrain on the head. "Good luck!" he chuckled to Devon.

Back in his apartment and bed, visions of swirling colors and flying above the clouds filled his head as he drifted off to sleep.

The next morning, Jeremy awoke wondering if it had all been a dream. But his mom had turned on the T.V. and it was all over the news. The colors of Pena Palace had been restored. Jeremy smiled as he flopped back onto his pillow.

"Time to get up, sleepy head. We're meeting Devon and her parents for breakfast before they have to leave to catch their flight."

In fifteen minutes, Jeremy was dressed and ready to go, Thing clipped once again to the belt loop of his jeans. Devon's family was waiting outside for them and they walked together to a restaurant around the corner, Devon and Jeremy trailing behind.

"I'm afraid Birdbrain is going to get caught!" Devon told Jeremy. "She won't stop flapping her wings and making noises."

"Perhaps she needs to be reminded to settle down," Jeremy laughed.

"She won't stop making farting noises! My parents keep looking at me strangely," Devon continued.

"You need to apologize," Thing chimed in.

"Whatever for?" Devon asked.

"You yelled at her," Thing replied.

"I what?" she said, stopping in the middle of the sidewalk.

"You yelled at her, when we were with the horseman. She was finally not afraid and you yelled at her. We magic buddies can be very sensitive, you know."

"It's true," Jeremy nodded, unsuccessfully stifling a laugh.

"Sorry, Birdbrain."

"Say it like you mean it," she replied.

Her cheeks turning a light shade of pink, Devon unclipped Birdbrain, held her up to her face and said, "I'm sorry for yelling at you."

"And it won't happen…" Birdbrain started.

"And it won't happen again," Devon said.

"Are you kids coming or what," Devon's mom called back to them.

"Coming," they both replied.

Devon clipped Birdbrain back on to her belt loop and they ran to catch up to their parents.

As everyone was finishing breakfast, Jeremy noticed that Devon was, again, twirling her hair, but he couldn't read the expression on her face.

"What's up?" he asked.

"What do you mean?"

"You twirl your hair when you're thinking about something."

"I do not," Devon said. "Hey!" She peered down at Birdbrain who had kicked her. Birdbrain nodded her head.

Laughing Jeremy asked again, "So, what's up?"

"Fine," she sighed. "I was wondering if you'd be up to writing, you know, emailing every now and then."

"Of course. You can tell me how you and your quiet buddy there are getting along," he chuckled.

Devon threw her napkin at Jeremy.

As they left the restaurant Devon turned and gave Jeremy a hug. "Don't forget to write," she said.

"I won't. And have fun with Birdbrain," he chuckled. Devon and her parents went back to their apartment to grab their bags before heading to the airport. Jeremy and his mom went about exploring more of Lisbon, leaving for home two days later.

As Jeremy packed his toy Tram 28 in his suitcase with the riddle re-taped to the bottom, he thought about all that Devon and he had done. It was a trip he wouldn't soon forget. "Where are we going next?" Thing asked as they were leaving the apartment.

"Home."

"No, after that?" Thing asked.

"That's a good question, buddy. Wherever it is, let's hope we get to go soon."